The Party Fairies

For Saoirse Medway

Special thanks to
Sue Mongredien

ORCHARD BOOKS
338 Euston Road, London NW1 3BH
Orchard Books Australia
Level 17/207 Kent Street, Sydney, NSW 2000
First published in 2005 by Orchard Books
© 2007 Rainbow Magic Limited
Rainbow Magic is a registered trademark
Illustrations © Georgie Ripper 2005
The right of Georgie Ripper to be identified as the illustrator
of this work has been asserted by her in accordance
with the Copyright, Designs and Patents Act, 1988.
A CIP catalogue record for this book is available
from the British Library.
ISBN 978 1 84362 818 7
1 3 5 7 9 10 8 6 4 2
Printed and bound in China
Orchard Books is a division of Hachette Children's Books,
an Hachette Livre UK company.
www.orchardbooks.co.uk

Cherry the Cake Fairy

by Daisy Meadows

illustrated by Georgie Ripper

ORCHARD BOOKS

www.rainbowmagic.co.uk

A Very Special Party Invitation

Our gracious King and gentle Queen
Are loved by fairies all.
One thousand years have they ruled well,
Through troubles great and small.

In honour of their glorious reign
A party has been planned,
To celebrate their jubilee
Throughout all Fairyland.

The party is a royal surprise,
We hope they'll be delighted.
So shine your wand and press your dress...
For you have been invited!

RSVP: HRH THE FAIRY GODMOTHER

Contents

A Birthday Surprise

"I just know this is going to be
a wonderful birthday!" Kirsty Tate
exclaimed happily, her eyes shining.

Mrs Tate laughed across the breakfast
table. "You've only been awake
for half an hour, Kirsty," she said.

"I know," Kirsty replied. "But
look at all these cards I've been sent!

And there's my party this afternoon. And best of all, Rachel's here for a whole week!" She grinned at her best

friend, Rachel Walker, who was sitting next to her. The two girls were spending a week of the Easter holidays together. They had met on holiday the year before and, since then, they had had all kinds of magical adventures together. First, they had helped all seven of the Rainbow Fairies return to Fairyland. Then, they'd helped the Weather Fairies stop wicked Jack Frost from causing weather chaos!

The girls finished their breakfast and
went to get dressed. Rachel was
halfway up the stairs behind Kirsty,
when she noticed another envelope
coming through the letterbox. She ran
to get it. It was a very grand-looking,
sparkly gold envelope, and it felt heavy
in her hand. She glanced at the front
curiously – and then gasped in surprise.

*Miss Kirsty Tate and Miss Rachel
Walker*, the beautiful loopy
handwriting read.
Rachel blinked.
A card for Kirsty
and for her?
It wasn't
her birthday
for another
three months!

She raced up the stairs, two at a time, puzzling it over. She didn't recognise the handwriting, so it couldn't be from her mum or dad. But who else knew that she was staying with Kirsty?

"Look," cried Rachel, bursting into Kirsty's bedroom. "Another card – and it's for both of us!"

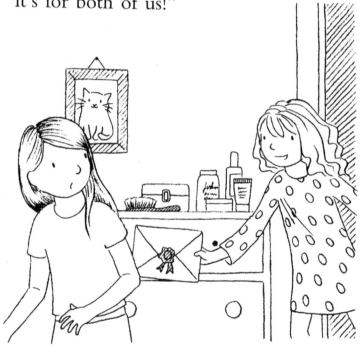

Kirsty took the envelope and gently turned it over, running her finger around the red wax seal on the back. "You open it," she said, passing the letter back to Rachel. "I've had all my other cards this morning."

Rachel's fingers trembled with excitement as she carefully broke the wax seal. As soon as the envelope was open, glittering clouds of fairy dust billowed into the air, followed by a rainbow of colour that soared across the room.

Both girls stared, open-mouthed. Riding on top of the rainbow, just as if he was surfing on a wave, was Bertram, the Fairyland frog footman! Rachel and Kirsty had met him before in their fairy adventures. But they hadn't expected to see him again in Kirsty's bedroom.

Bertram hopped off the rainbow onto Kirsty's chest of drawers and bowed deeply. He wore a red waistcoat and carried a gold bugle.

Kirsty grabbed Rachel's hand excitedly and squeezed it. She couldn't help wondering if this would be the start of another magical quest!

Bertram tooted on the bugle, then
pulled a tiny scroll from one of his
pockets. He unrolled it, and cleared his
throat. "Ahem. It is with great
pleasure," he began,
"that I bring you
good news. The
Fairy Godmother
hereby invites
Kirsty Tate and
Rachel Walker to a
surprise party – for
the Fairy King and
Queen's 1000th jubilee!"
"Wow!" gasped Rachel.
"Yes, please!" Kirsty cried.
From another of his pockets, Bertram
pulled out a tiny bag of fairy dust and
began sprinkling it over Kirsty's mirror.

As the girls watched, the mirror's reflection vanished and a whole new scene appeared before their eyes.

"It's Fairyland!" Rachel breathed, leaning closer for a better look.

"Correct," said Bertram. "The Fairy Party Workshop, to be precise. All the Party Fairies have been working very hard to make sure the King and Queen's party is absolutely perfect."

Kirsty and Rachel gazed in delight at the small figures they could see bustling around in the workshop.

17

"There's Cherry the Cake Fairy, making
a special party cake," Bertram told
them, pointing a webbed green
finger. The cake did
indeed look wonderful.
It was shaped like a fairy
palace and it sparkled
with magic. "That's
Grace the Glitter Fairy,
making lots of magical
decorations. And can
you see the fairy
wrapping up gifts so
prettily? She's Jasmine
the Present Fairy."

The two girls watched in
delight as Jasmine tied a pink satin
bow around one of the presents.
"Who else is there?" Kirsty asked eagerly.

Bertram pointed. "There's Polly the Party Fun Fairy. She's in charge of party games. And Melodie the Music Fairy sorts out the best party tunes. She's teaching the fairy orchestra how to play the harmonies for 'Happy Jubilee'."

The girls fell silent and listened to the sweet sounds of fairy music tinkling through the mirror. "It's gorgeous," Rachel sighed.

Bertram went on. "Honey the Sweet Fairy is making sure there are enough treats to go round, and Phoebe the Fashion Fairy – she's the one with the extra-sparkly wings, look – is in charge of everybody's party outfits."

Kirsty gazed in wonder at the
beautiful dress Phoebe was working on.
It was covered with hundreds of sequins
and jewels that glittered in the light.
"It's lovely," breathed Kirsty, her eyes
wide with excitement. "And we're
really invited to the party?"

"Oh, yes," Bertram replied. "The
Fairy Godmother says that you and
Rachel will be special guests."

"Special guests!" Rachel echoed,
looking thrilled at the thought.

"So, when is the party? And how will we get there?" Kirsty asked.

Bertram murmured something at the mirror and the Fairyland scene dissolved into hundreds of twinkling stars, before finally disappearing.

"The party's at the end of the week. And the Fairy Godmother will send a magic rainbow to collect you," he said. He handed the magic invitation to Rachel. "To get to Fairyland, all you have to do is step into the end of the rainbow," he explained, "like this."

Kirsty and Rachel watched as
Bertram placed one froggy foot,
then another, into the colourful
rainbow that hovered in the air.
And then – *whoosh* – with a shower
of golden fairy dust, he was gone.

"Hurrah!" exclaimed Kirsty. "I knew this was going to be a brilliant birthday."

Fun and Games

Rachel and Kirsty got dressed, chatting excitedly.

"'Special guests', the Fairy Godmother called us," Rachel said proudly, tying up her hair in a band. "Imagine! You and me, special guests of the Fairy King and Queen!"

25

"It's amazing," Kirsty grinned, brushing her hair. "I can't wait to go to Fairyland again."

Just then, there was a shout from downstairs. "Come on, girls!" Mrs Tate called. "There's lots to do before the party starts."

Rachel and Kirsty looked at each other in amazement. How did Mrs Tate know about the Fairyland party? Then Kirsty chuckled. "She means my party," she said. "Do you know, I'd almost forgotten all about it!"

The girls laughed and hurried downstairs. In the kitchen, Mr Tate was icing Kirsty's birthday cake. "There," he said, putting nine candles on top. "It's all finished."

"That looks delicious, Dad," Kirsty said, hugging him. "Come on, Rachel – let's see what Mum wants us to do."

Mrs Tate soon had the two girls making up party bags for all of Kirsty's guests. Then they blew up lots of pink and lilac balloons to hang from the ceiling. And finally there was just time for the girls to put on their party dresses before the guests arrived.

"Musical Statues first," Mrs Tate announced to all the girls gathered in the

lounge. "When the music stops – so do you!" The music started and everybody danced. Then Mr Tate switched it off – and everybody froze on the spot. Rachel was standing on one leg, trying to keep as still as possible, when she suddenly saw swirls of red and purple glitter floating through the doorway. She stared in surprise, wondering what it could be.

Then she flicked her eyes to the side, wondering if Kirsty had spotted the glitter, too. Kirsty's startled expression told Rachel that she had, but none of the other children seemed to have noticed anything unusual.

The sparkling dust floated up to Rachel, drifting right under her nose. "Atishoo! Atishoo! Atishoo!" she sneezed.

Now the dust was under Kirsty's nose, too. It was so ticklish, she just couldn't help rubbing her nose.

"Rachel and Kirsty – you two are out!" Mrs Tate said. "Here comes the music again."

As quickly as they had appeared, the
swirls of red and purple glitter vanished.
Rachel frowned at Kirsty. "What
was that?" she hissed as they went
to sit down.

Kirsty grabbed her arm and steered
her towards the door. "I think it
might have had something to do
with her," she whispered, pointing
through the doorway.

Rachel followed Kirsty's finger, and a broad smile spread over her face. For there, hovering in mid-air and waving at the girls, was a tiny sparkling fairy!

Stop Thief!

"You're one of the Party Fairies!"
Rachel exclaimed as they rushed over to
speak to the fairy. "We saw you in
Bertram's picture."

The fairy smiled. She had lovely, deep
violet eyes and long, dark, curly hair,
tied in bunches with red ribbons. She
wore a red skirt, a pink wrap-around

top, red party shoes and stripy socks.
From her wrist, swung a sparkly red
party bag. "I certainly am," she replied,
with a little curtsey. "I'm Cherry the
Cake Fairy."

An anxious
frown creased
her forehead.
"I'm sorry if my
fairy dust spoiled
your game," she went on,
"but I really need your help!"

"Of course!" Kirsty said at once.

"Whatever's happened?" Rachel asked.

Cherry smiled gratefully. "Well, you
see, as the Cake Fairy, whenever a party
is in danger of being ruined by a spoiled
cake, I get called away from Fairyland
to fix it. And today, I've been very busy.

One of Jack Frost's goblins has been spoiling birthday cakes all over the country. He steals the cake candles, and stomps in the icing." She bit her lip. "And he's on his way to Kirsty's party right now!"

Rachel's mouth fell open. "What a cheek!" she exclaimed.

Kirsty glanced over to the kitchen door. "Why is the goblin spoiling all the cakes?" she asked. "And what can we do to stop him?"

Cherry's eyes flashed. "Nobody knows what the goblin is up to," she told the girls. "But one thing's for sure − if Jack Frost's behind it, it's bound to be something bad." She shrugged. "All we can do is try to catch the goblin before he causes any more trouble."

"What are we waiting for?" Rachel cried. "Let's stand guard over Kirsty's cake at once!"

The girls raced to the kitchen, with Cherry fluttering along behind. As soon as they opened the kitchen door, though, they knew that they were too late. All the candles had been pulled out of Kirsty's cake, and there were goblin footprints in the icing.

"Oh, no!" cried Kirsty in dismay. "He's ruined it!"

"He's taken all the candles, too,"
Rachel added crossly.

"And I'll take this, as well!" they
heard somebody cackle. And before
anyone could stop him, a grinning
green goblin jumped out from behind
one of the table legs, snatched Cherry's
party bag out of her hands and ran off,
laughing nastily.

A Tricky Problem

"Hey!" Cherry cried. "Give that back!"

Kirsty and Rachel stared in horror as the goblin ran away. He was his normal size, Rachel noted with relief. She remembered that the Fairy King and Queen had taken Jack Frost's magic away for one year, after his mean mischief had nearly ruined Christmas.

Clearly, his punishment meant that he hadn't been able to cast a spell to make the goblins super-sized like he'd done once before. An enormous rucksack bumped up and down on the goblin's back. It was stuffed full of party candles.

"We've got to get my party bag back!" Cherry cried, flying after the thief. "Quick!"

The goblin was just about to dodge
out of the kitchen door, when Kirsty's
kitten, Pearl, came bounding into the
room. As soon as Pearl saw the goblin,
she fluffed up her black and white fur in
alarm and hissed.

The goblin's eyes
bulged in panic and
he skidded to a
halt. Then he
climbed up to
one of the kitchen
cupboards and
locked himself in!

Cherry flitted about anxiously. "That
party bag has got all my magical fairy
dust inside," she fretted. "I need that to
help make parties perfect – and to finish
off the King and Queen's jubilee cake."

Rachel banged on the cupboard door. "Give that party bag back to Cherry this minute!" she ordered the goblin.

"No chance," the goblin shouted back sulkily. "It's mine now – and as soon as I get out of here, I'll be giving it to Jack Frost."

"What does he want it for?" Kirsty asked curiously.

The goblin gave a gloating chuckle. "For his party of course," he replied. "The King and Queen said he's got to stay in his ice castle, but they didn't say he couldn't have a party – and a very grand one it's going to be, too!

Now that I've got this party bag of magic dust, his cake is going to be the most splendid cake you ever saw." There was another cackle of glee from the cupboard. "Just you wait – once we've got all the Party Fairies' party bags, Jack Frost will use the magic dust, instead of his own magic, to make his party extra-special."

Cherry had turned quite pale. She beckoned the girls back over to the table, where they huddled together to hear her whisper.

"It's bad enough that he's got my party bag when I haven't finished the King and Queen's cake," she said. "But if the goblins are planning to steal all the magical party bags, then none of the Party Fairies will be able to finish their work in time for the jubilee."

She shook her head miserably. "The surprise party will be ruined!"

A Sticky Solution

The girls thought hard to try and find a way of recovering Cherry's party bag. But they couldn't think of anything.

"The Fairy Godmother is much more powerful than a goblin," Cherry sighed. "She'd soon sort all this out if only I could get the goblin back to Fairyland.

But I can't magic him there while he's in that cupboard – or while he's running away. I need him to keep fairly still, so that I can wave my wand over him."

Kirsty found her gaze drifting towards her ruined birthday cake. "Poor Dad spent ages on that icing," she said sadly.

Then she grinned suddenly as a thought struck her. "That's it!" she muttered. "That's how we'll catch him out!"

"How?" Rachel asked blankly.

"We need to make more icing for this cake," Kirsty said loudly. She took out a box of icing sugar and started mixing some icing in a bowl.

Then she added quietly, "Cherry, could you use some fairy magic to make this icing extra-sticky?"

"No problem," Cherry replied. She waved her wand over the bowl and a stream of sparkling purple and red fairy dust swirled around it. The white icing glittered for a split-second and strange red and purple sparks crackled above it. Then it turned a glossy white again.

Kirsty gave one last stir and smiled. "Super-sticky!" she whispered.

Rachel was still frowning. "I don't—" she began.

But Kirsty put a finger to her lips. "It's a trap!" she whispered into Rachel's ear. Quickly, she covered the cake with the new icing. "We'd better get back to the party now that the cake's all right again. We'll just leave it here on the table..." she said loudly.

Rachel and Cherry
followed Kirsty
out of the room.
Holding their breath,
they waited outside the
kitchen, peeping through
the crack in the door to
see if Kirsty's trap would work.
Sure enough, after a moment, the
cupboard door creaked open
and the goblin climbed
down and skipped
gleefully across
the floor. Grinning
nastily, he climbed
up onto the kitchen
table, and then made
a massive leap straight
onto the top of the newly-iced cake.

"There he goes," Kirsty whispered to Rachel. "And any second now, he'll realise..."

"I'm stuck!" the goblin howled suddenly. "They've tricked me!"

"Perfect timing," chuckled Cherry.

The goblin was stuck fast, unable to move his feet in the super-sticky icing. Rachel laughed out loud at his furious face. "Brilliant idea, Kirsty," she cheered.

Cherry flew over to the goblin,
her eyes on her precious
party bag, but he
bared his teeth at
her. "Any closer,
fairy, and
I'll bite you!"
he warned.

"In that case,
I'll have to
take you back
to Fairyland,"
Cherry said calmly.
"And won't the Fairy Godmother be
interested to hear what you and Jack
Frost have been plotting?"

The goblin scowled, but said no more.

"Serves you right for ruining my
cake – twice!" Kirsty couldn't help adding.

"Don't worry about your cake, Kirsty," Cherry said. "Once I've got my party bag back, I'll magic you the most beautiful birthday cake you've ever seen. Now, I don't suppose you two would like to come to Fairyland with me, would you?"

"Yes, please!" Kirsty cried at once, but Rachel was glancing up at the kitchen clock.

"What about your party, Kirsty?" she pointed out. "Musical Statues must be about to end soon."

Cherry twirled her wand around. "Don't worry," she said, "I'll work some magic so that it will seem as if you've only been gone from the party for a moment. Will that help?"

"Oh, yes!" cried both girls together.

"I was hoping you'd say that," Cherry smiled. "Off we go!"

every time they moved. Her long
golden dress was covered in tiny
glimmering jewels that twinkled all
the colours of the rainbow.

"I'm Kirsty," Kirsty said, jumping
up at once.

"And I'm Rachel," Rachel added,
scrambling to her feet.

"Delighted to meet you at last,"
the Fairy Godmother replied,
dropping a beautiful curtsey.

Then her eyes narrowed at the sight of the goblin, standing next to Cherry. "I see that you've taken something that doesn't belong to you," she said sternly, pointing a finger at Cherry's party bag.

Whizz! The party bag glowed with red and purple light and shot out of the goblin's hands at once. It zoomed straight over to Cherry, who clutched it with relief.

"Thank you!" she cried.

"You're welcome, my dear," the Fairy Godmother said. Then she fixed

60

her gaze on the goblin. "As for you, I've got just the thing to teach you a lesson." She pointed a finger at him. "You'll need that," she said, "and that."

Kirsty and Rachel couldn't help laughing as an enormous chef's hat suddenly appeared on the goblin's head, and a crisp white apron wrapped itself around his body.

"You can help in the Party Workshop for the rest of the week, icing all the cakes," the Fairy Godmother went on firmly.

"Let's hope that keeps you out of mischief."

The goblin looked very sulky as Cherry bustled him away. "You won't catch the other goblins so easily," he snarled. "We'll get the rest of those party bags, just you wait and see!"

Once he'd gone, the Fairy Godmother turned back to Kirsty and Rachel. "I'm afraid he might be right," she told them. "Jack Frost's goblins can be very cunning, as you know. They'll try every trick they can think of to steal the other magical party bags."

"What can we do to help?" Kirsty asked at once.

The Fairy Godmother smiled and sighed. "All you can do is look out for trouble at parties," she said. "The goblins are likely to try and spoil human parties because they know that the Party Fairies will rush to help.

That will give them the chance they need to steal the fairies' party bags."

"We'll keep a look-out," Rachel promised.

At that moment, Cherry returned. "We'd better send you back to your party," she told the girls. "And don't worry – I'm sure there won't be any more goblins to spoil your fun today." She carefully opened her party bag and reached inside. Then, just as the

Fairy Godmother pointed her wand at the girls and called, "Home!" Cherry threw a handful of red and purple fairy dust over them.

The world seemed to spin, there was a sweet, sugary smell in the air and then the girls found themselves back in Kirsty's kitchen.

"Jessica's the winner!" they heard Mrs Tate saying. "Come and get your prize for being the best statue, Jessica."

"It sounds like the game's only just finished," Kirsty said happily. "Just like Cherry promised. Let's go and join the party again, Rachel."

But Rachel was staring at the kitchen table in wonder. "Look, Kirsty!" she gulped. "Look at your cake!"

Kirsty gasped in surprise. The red and purple fairy dust that Cherry had thrown over them was floating down onto the cake that Mr Tate had made. As the girls watched, they realised that the fairy dust was actually red and purple hundreds and thousands, and as they landed on the cake something amazing happened. A delicious fragrance of vanilla and sugar floated around the room, and the original cake melted into thin air, while a new cake formed in its place. Kirsty and Rachel stared in wonder as three tiers appeared, one by one, beautifully covered with white, pink and lilac icing. Each tier was decorated with tiny sugar fairies, twining sugar roses and shiny silver bells. Kirsty broke the silence with a sudden laugh. "It's the Party Fairies!" she cried, pointing at the sugar figures. "There's Cherry with a wooden spoon, see? And the Glitter Fairy, didn't Bertram say her name was Grace? And a fairy with a present – that must be Jasmine. And— "

Suddenly, they heard Mrs Tate calling for them. "Kirsty! Rachel! Where are you?"

"Time to go," Rachel said. "Shall we take the cake in with us, just to be on the safe side?"

"Good idea," said Kirsty. Then she grinned. "I can't wait to see everybody's faces!"

Very carefully, the girls lifted the magnificent cake. As they carried it into the living room together, the little silver bells tinkled merrily.

"Wow!" cried Kirsty's friend Jessica. "I've never seen anything like it."

Another girl, Molly, was licking her lips. "It's almost too beautiful to eat," she said. "Although it smells so gorgeous, I'll give it a try!"

Mrs Tate looked dazzled. "It's a work of art!" she said to her husband in amazement.

Mr Tate was staring at the cake, too, with a bewildered expression on his face. "Well... Um... It's not so difficult when you know how," he said sheepishly.

"I can't wait to see what you're going to do for my birthday next month!" Mrs Tate added. Mr Tate looked rather alarmed at that, so Kirsty interrupted quickly.

"Shall we cut the cake, Mum?"

"Good idea," Mrs Tate replied. She lit the candles, and everybody sang 'Happy Birthday'. Then Kirsty carefully sliced into the lowest tier of the cake.

As she did so, hundreds of magical butterflies fluttered out into the room, their colourful wings sparkling in the sunshine.

"Ooooh!" everybody exclaimed, as the butterflies vanished into thin air. "Just like magic!"

Kirsty and Rachel smiled at each other. They both knew that it *was* magic – fairy magic, the most wonderful magic in all the world!

As they tucked into slices of the delicious birthday cake, they both thought of their new fairy mission with excitement.

"I can't wait to meet the other Party Fairies," Rachel whispered to Kirsty. "But I'm not looking forward to seeing any more goblins."

"I know," Kirsty agreed. "I just hope we can stop them from spoiling the King and Queen's party."

Rachel patted her friend's arm comfortingly. "At least Cherry said there'd be no more trouble at your party," she pointed out. "So we can enjoy the rest of your birthday without worrying."

Kirsty nodded. "Yes," she said. Then she grinned. "An invitation to the King and Queen's jubilee party, meeting Cherry and a visit to Fairyland – I just knew this was going to be a wonderful birthday," she sighed happily, "and I was right."

The Party Fairies

Cherry has got her magic
party bag back. Now Rachel
and Kirsty must help

Melodie the Music Fairy

Win a Rainbow Magic
Sparkly T-Shirt and Goody Bag!

In every book in the Rainbow Magic Party Fairies series (books 15-21) there is a hidden picture of a magic party bag with a secret letter in it. Find all seven letters and re-arrange them to make a special Fairyland word, then send it to us. Each month we will put the entries into a draw and select one winner to receive a Rainbow Magic Sparkly T-shirt and Goody Bag!

Send your entry on a postcard to Rainbow Magic Competition, Orchard Books, 96 Leonard Street, London EC2A 4XD. Australian readers should write to 32/45-51 Huntley Street, Alexandria, NSW 2015. Don't forget to include your name and address. Only one entry per child. Final draw: 28th April 2006.

Coming Soon...
The Jewel Fairies

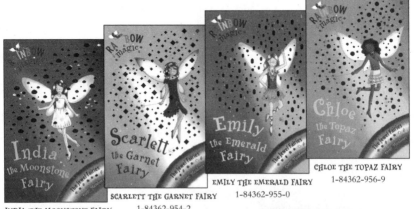

INDIA THE MOONSTONE FAIRY
1-84362-958-5

SCARLETT THE GARNET FAIRY   1-84362-954-2

EMILY THE EMERALD FAIRY
1-84362-955-0

CHLOE THE TOPAZ FAIRY
1-84362-956-9

AMY THE AMETHYST FAIRY
1-84362-957-7

SOPHIE THE SAPPHIRE FAIRY
1-84362-953-4

LUCY THE DIAMOND FAIRY
1-84362-959-3

Also coming soon . . .

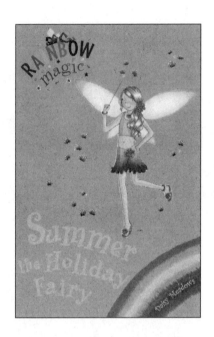

SUMMER THE HOLIDAY FAIRY

1-84362-638-1

Summer the Holiday Fairy is getting all hot and bothered, trying to keep Rainspell Island the best place to go on vacation. Jack Frost has stolen the sand from the beaches, and three magical shells. The fairies need Rachel and Kirsty's help to get the holiday magic back...

Have you checked out the

Website at:

www.rainbowmagic.co.uk

There are games, activities and
fun things to do, as well as news
and information about Rainbow
Magic and all of the fairies.

RAINBOW magic

by Daisy Meadows

Ruby the Red Fairy	ISBN	1 84362 016 2
Amber the Orange Fairy	ISBN	1 84362 017 0
Saffron the Yellow Fairy	ISBN	1 84362 018 9
Fern the Green Fairy	ISBN	1 84362 019 7
Sky the Blue Fairy	ISBN	1 84362 020 0
Izzy the Indigo Fairy	ISBN	1 84362 021 9
Heather the Violet Fairy	ISBN	1 84362 022 7

The Weather Fairies

Crystal the Snow Fairy	ISBN	1 84362 633 0
Abigail the Breeze Fairy	ISBN	1 84362 634 9
Pearl the Cloud Fairy	ISBN	1 84362 635 7
Goldie the Sunshine Fairy	ISBN	1 84362 641 1
Evie the Mist Fairy	ISBN	1 84362 636 5
Storm the Lightning Fairy	ISBN	1 84362 637 3
Hayley the Rain Fairy	ISBN	1 84362 638 1

The Party Fairies

Cherry the Cake Fairy	ISBN	1 84362 818 X
Melodie the Music Fairy	ISBN	1 84362 819 8
Grace the Glitter Fairy	ISBN	1 84362 820 1
Honey the Sweet Fairy	ISBN	1 84362 821 X
Polly the Party Fun Fairy	ISBN	1 84362 822 8
Phoebe the Fashion Fairy	ISBN	1 84362 823 6
Jasmine the Present Fairy	ISBN	1 84362 824 4
Holly the Christmas Fairy	ISBN	1 84362 661 6

All priced at £3.99. Holly the Christmas Fairy priced at £4.99.
Rainbow Magic books are available from all good bookshops, or can be ordered
direct from the publisher: Orchard Books, PO BOX 29, Douglas IM99 1BQ
Credit card orders please telephone 01624 836000
or fax 01624 837033 or visit our Internet site: www.wattspub.co.uk
or e-mail: bookshop@enterprise.net for details.

To order please quote title, author and ISBN and your full name and address.
Cheques and postal orders should be made payable to 'Bookpost plc.'
Postage and packing is FREE within the UK
(overseas customers should add £2.00 per book).
Prices and availability are subject to change.